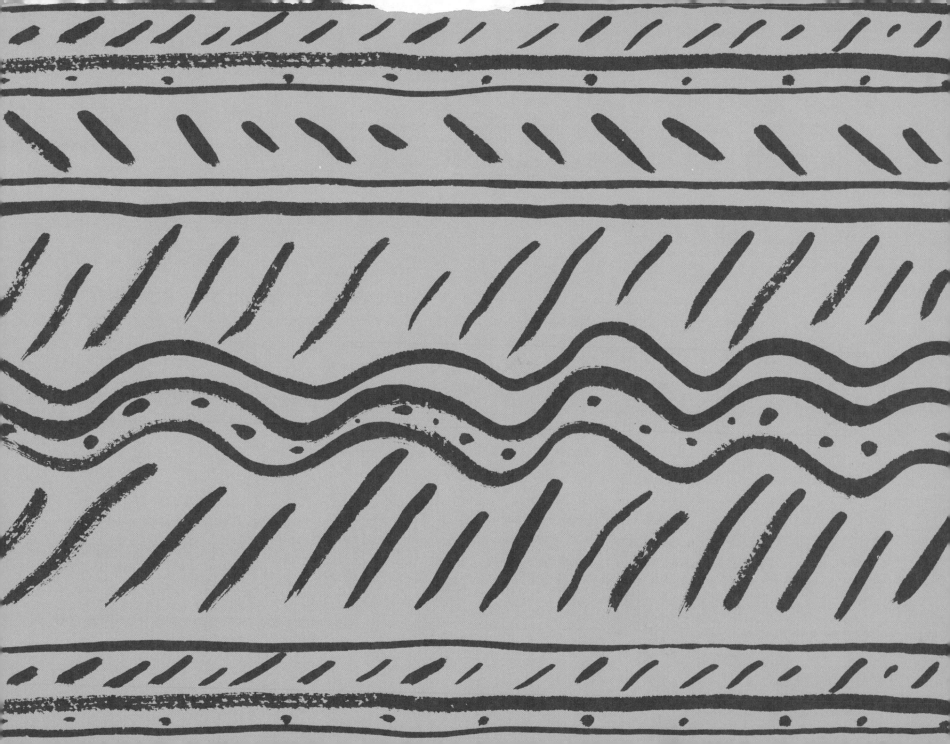

IMANI'S MOON

JaNay Brown-Wood

Illustrated by Hazel Mitchell

To those who dream big and aim high

—J. B.-W.

For Ashley, for all the courage, and for Lizzie

—H. M.

Established in 1921, the National Association of Elementary School Principals (NAESP) leads in the advocacy and support for elementary- and middle-level principals in the United States, Canada, and overseas. The NAESP Foundation, founded in 1982, is the charitable arm of NAESP and is dedicated to securing and stewarding private gifts and grants that benefit NAESP.

Imani's Moon
Text copyright © 2014 by JaNay Brown-Wood
Illustrations copyright © 2014 by Hazel Mitchell

A Mackinac Island Book
Published by Charlesbridge, 85 Main Street, Watertown, MA 02472
(617) 926-0329 • www.charlesbridge.com

Library of Congress Cataloging-in-Publication Data
Brown-Wood, JaNay.
Imani's moon/JaNay Brown-Wood; illustrated by Hazel Mitchell.
    p. cm
    Summary: Little Imani of the Maasai people longs to do something great, like touching the moon, but the other children just laugh at her.
    ISBN 978-1-934133-57-6 (reinforced for library use)
    ISBN 978-1-934133-58-3 (softcover)
    ISBN 978-1-60734-753-8 (ebook)
    ISBN 978-1-60734-705-7 (ebook pdf)
1. Maasai (African people)—Juvenile fiction. 2. Belief and doubt—Juvenile fiction. 3. Self-confidence—Juvenile fiction. 4. Moon—Juvenile fiction. [1. Maasai (African people)—Fiction. 2. Belief and doubt—Fiction. 3. Self-confidence—Fiction. 4. Moon—Fiction. 5. Blacks—Africa—Fiction.] I. Mitchell, Hazel ill. II. Title.
PZ7.B81983Im 2014
[E]—dc23   2013033433

Printed in China
(hc) 10 9 8 7 6 5 4 3 2 1
(sc) 10 9 8 7 6 5 4 3 2 1

Illustrations created with watercolor and graphite then over-painted digitally
Display type set in P22 Eaglefeather
Text type set in Goudy
Printed by Jade Productions in Heyuan, Guangdong, China
Production supervision by Brian G. Walker
Designed by Susan Mallory Sherman

IMANI was the smallest child in her village.

"Look at tiny Imani!" the other children teased. "She's no higher than a lion cub's knee!"

"Careful," they called to her. "Don't let the meerkats stomp on your head!"

"Mini Imani, you'll never accomplish anything!"
Day in and day out, the children teased her,
and Imani began to believe them.

Every night Imani's mama lifted her spirits with stories. This night Mama told her of Olapa, the goddess of the moon who fought a great battle against the god of the sun and triumphed.

"Do you think I could do something great like Olapa?" asked Imani.

"I do," answered Mama.

"Even something like touching the moon?"

"Even that," said Mama. "But it is you who must believe."

Mama kissed her forehead. "*Usiku mwema.* Good night, Imani."

"Good night, Mama."

That night Olapa and Imani battled side by side in Imani's dreams. Together they protected the people of earth from danger, flew through the sky, and guarded the moon. Imani stood tall and brave on the moon with Olapa beside her.

The next morning Imani awoke, inspired to do something great.

"Today," she told herself, "I will touch the moon."

Later that day Imani made her way through the village. "Look! It's Imani the Ant," called one of the teasing children.

"Where are you off to?" teased another. "Going to catch a ride on a beetle's back?"

"I am going to touch the moon," answered Imani. The children laughed and followed her.

As the moon grew brighter in the late-day sky, Imani began to climb the tallest tree. The bark scraped her small hands and legs.

On a branch above, Nyoka the snake appeared.

"What'sss going on?" he hissed.

"I am going to touch the moon," answered Imani.

"That's imposssssible!" Nyoka jeered. "It's much too high!"

Imani climbed on.

As she got higher and higher, climbing became harder and harder.

She stretched herself to reach the next branch but lost her footing and fell to the ground with a . . .

THUMP!

"Maybe I won't touch the moon." She sighed.

That night Mama told Imani about Anansi, the small spider who captured a snake to gain a name for himself.

"Mama, do you believe that a spider, so small and weak, could really capture a snake, so long and quick?" Imani asked.

"I do," answered Mama.

"Even if no one else believes it?" Imani asked.

"A challenge is only impossible until someone accomplishes it," Mama said. "Imani, it is only *you* who must believe."

Imani drifted to sleep and dreamed that *she* climbed to the top of the highest tree in her village, captured a snake, and made a name for herself.

The next day Imani searched the village and gathered twigs, leaves, sticky berries, and rope. Then she headed back to the tallest tree, sat down, and got to work.

"What's Imani the Tiny up to today?" teased the children.

"I am going to touch the moon," Imani answered.

As the moon began to appear, Imani pulled her creation onto her arms. She spread her arms out wide and sprinted past the tallest tree as quickly as she could.

Imani's wings caught a gust of wind. She soared as high as the treetops.

"What are you-ooh doing up here?" asked Sokwe the chimpanzee, confused to see a flying human.

"I am going to touch the moon!" Imani called

"You-ooh can't do-ooh that! Give up! Give up!" mocked Sokwe.

Imani flew on. Then suddenly a strong burst of wind—too mighty for her delicate wings—sent her sailing into the tree with a . . .

CRASH!

The children laughed and left her behind.
"I give up." She sighed.

Heading back home Imani heard her village gathered in celebration. The young warriors were performing the *adumu*, the jumping dance. Over and over again the warriors jumped high into the sky, their heads caressing the clouds. Cheers and chants rang from the proud villagers. One of the warriors jumped higher than any other. This warrior seemed to fly. Imani could not look away. She cheered the loudest for him.

After the celebration Mama and Imani returned home. Too tired for a story, Imani went straight to sleep. Her dreams danced with visions of the *adumu*. The cheers and chants from her tribe still echoed in her head.

When morning broke, Imani went to the tallest tree.
The teasing children followed.
"She's going to climb again!" they hollered.
But instead, Imani jumped.

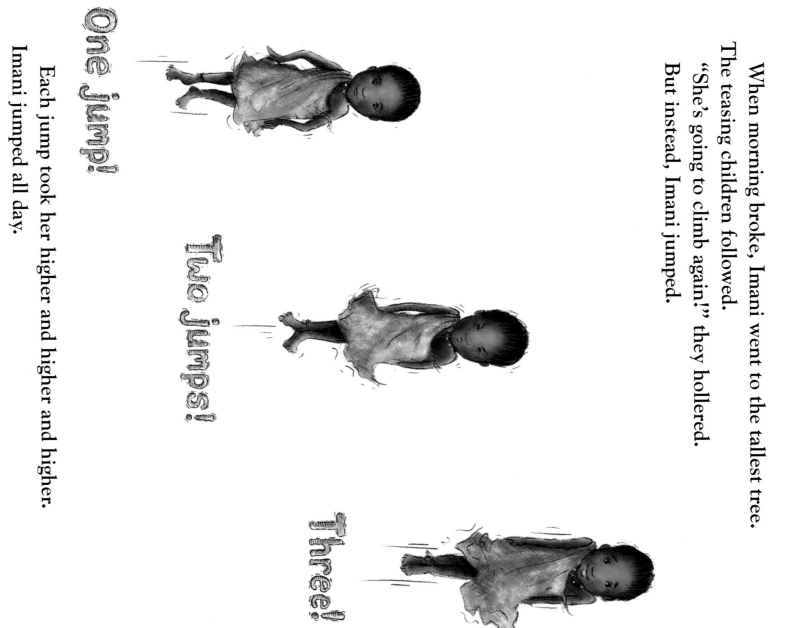

One jump!

Two jumps!

Three!

Each jump took her higher and higher and higher.
Imani jumped all day.

As the sky grew darker, Bundi the owl flew by. "What are you-hoo doing?" he asked.

"I am going to touch the moon," Imani answered

"Don't fool yourself. You-hoo won't make it!" hooted Bundi.

But Imani jumped on.

Her body grew tired. Her legs ached, her feet throbbed, and the children continued to taunt.

But like a warrior she jumped higher than each jump before. In her mind she could hear only the cheers and chants of her proud village. She could see only herself as one of the warriors, rising from the earth. She kept her eyes on the moon above and felt herself getting closer. With a final push of her legs, Imani jumped once more . . . .

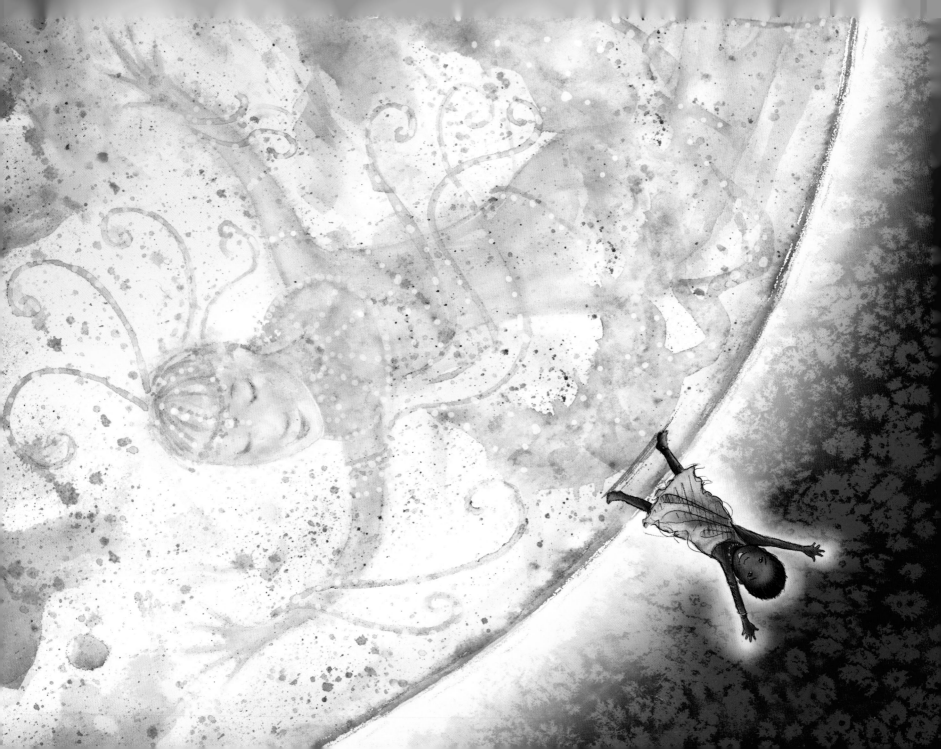

. . . and soared through the night sky.
She landed on the face of the moon.
"Olapa!" Imani called. "I am here! I am
I have made it to the moon!"
"So you have," said a voice in the wind. "Welcome."
Imani clapped. She laughed. She sang. She rolled in
the moon dust and danced with excitement. As she
celebrated she noticed something shiny.

She picked up the thing that dazzled her eye and turned it over in her hands. It was a small, round moon rock. Her own tiny moon.

"A gift for you, Imani the Great," said the voice.

"Thank you, Goddess of the Moon." Imani smiled.

Feeling lighter than ever before, Imani jumped one last time and floated from the moon toward the waiting earth.

Down from the sky came Imani, the small girl with the small moon in her hand. All was quiet. No one taunted or hissed or mocked or hooted.

That night Imani called to her mama. "Can I tell you a story tonight?" she asked.

"Which one?" asked Mama.

"It is *The Tale of the Girl Who Touched the Moon.*"

Mama listened as Imani told her story.

"Where did you hear such a tale?" asked Mama.

Imani opened her hands and revealed the glowing moon rock, so small and beautiful.

"It is my story, Mama," said Imani. "I am the girl who touched the moon and was welcomed by Olapa. I am the one who believed."

Author's Note

On the plains of Tanzania and Kenya live the Maasai people, an African tribe known for their bright robes and their cultural jumping dance called the *adumu* (ah-deh-moo). During the *adumu*, warriors from the tribe stand in a circle and try to outjump each other, leaping high with their strong legs while barely moving their arms. Sometimes the dance is done while the warriors chant or sing songs. This ritual reminds me of a beautiful and artistic ballet and compelled me to research the Maasai people through several documentaries, books, and photographs. I soon became inspired to write Imani's story.

Africa became an ideal setting—and the Maasai the perfect tribe—to nurture a strong and perseverant character like Imani. African people such as the Maasai have many cultural stories and mythologies that they pass on through spoken narratives. Imani's mother carries on this tradition by telling Imani of Olapa, the moon goddess of Maasai mythology, and of Anansi, the spider. Passing on stories to eager listeners is one reason why I became an author. Just as Imani enthusiastically passes her story on to Mama, I am thrilled to pass this one on to you.

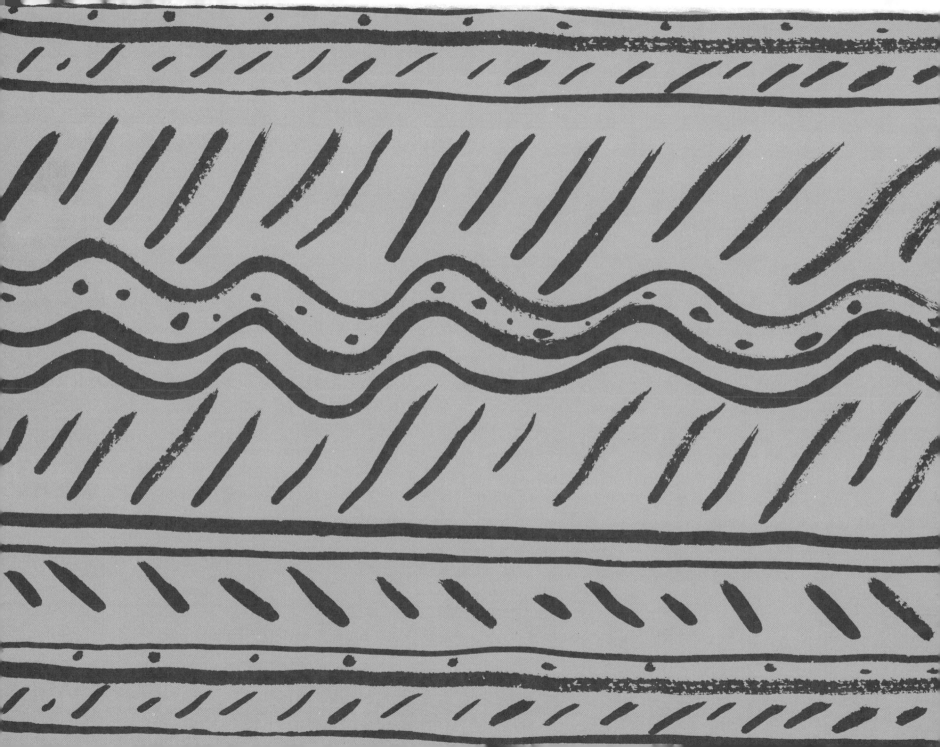